For my daughter, Emma, whose imagination brought us water chickens,
people crackers, and colored Cheerios.

I would like to say a massive thank-you to Jill Davis and Jeanne
Hogle, who made this book so much better than I ever could have.

Sheep Dog and Sheep Sheep: Baaad Hair Day
Copyright © 2020 by Eric Barclay
All rights reserved. Manufactured in China.
No part of this book may be used or reproduced in any manner whatsoever
without written permission except in the case of brief quotations
embodied in critical articles and reviews. For information address HarperCollins Children's Books,
a division of HarperCollins Publishers, 195 Broadway, New York, NY 10007.
www.harpercollinschildrens.com

ISBN: 978-0-06-267739-6

The artist used pencil and Adobe Photoshop to create the illustrations for this book.
Typography by Jeanne Hogle
20 21 22 23 24 SCP 10 9 8 7 6 5 4 3 2 1
❖
First Edition

SHEEP DOG AND SHEEP SHEEP
Baaad Hair Day

ERIC BARCLAY

HARPER
An Imprint of HarperCollinsPublishers

This is Sheep. She loves her naturally curly wool.

When it's full and fluffy, she feels as light as a cloud.

Sometimes she styles her wool in a bun, like this...

or ties it up into pigtails, like this...

or puts it in a fancy hairdo, like this.

But—oh no!—her
wool has grown too full...

and too fluffy.

And when it's this full and fluffy, she can't see.

And when she can't see, she trips over things—usually rocks.

SPLASH!

"Holy begonia!
Water chickens!"

"Good-bye, water chickens!"

"Hello, Sheep Dog!"

"How can I see with all this wool in my eyes?"

Sheep Dog had the answer.

"NO THANK YOU!"

Sheep replied.

Off Sheep went—past the tractor . . .

past the chickens . . .

through the cow poop . . .

past the well . . .

. . . and right into the mud.

But she meant to do that.
Really.

"Why didn't you look where
I was going?"

"You just need a haircut," said Sheep Dog.

"You'll feel so much better."

Sheep Dog ran to the old truck to see if Sheep was hiding there.

He looked in the meadow.

He looked in the shed.

He even asked the pig.

"Has anyone seen sheep?"
he asked at the duck pond.

"Nobody here but us water chickens," said a bush.

Finally, he found her.
"I'm just not ready to give up my fluffy wool," Sheep said sadly.